Bigfoot
and the
Michigamme Trolls

**Tales from the archives of the
Lake Ellen Hunting, Fishing,
Camping & Literary Society**

Compiled by Lloyd Mattson

Cover and illustrations by Harvey Sandstrom

The Wordshed ♦ ♦ Duluth, Minnesota

ISBN 0-942684-28-1

Copies available from
The Wordshed
5118 Glendale Street ♦ Duluth, MN 55804
218/525-3266 ♦ wordshed@charter.net

Printed in the United States of America

Arrow Printing ♦ ♦ Bemidji, Minnesota

Contents

*Remembering Darwin Wilson,
friend of kids and Lake Ellen Camp.*

Prologue

The stories in this small book came from the archives of the Lake Ellen Hunting, Fishing, Camping & Literary Society. Fact is, the stories *are* the archives. That's all she wrote. Like skit night at teen camp or broom ball at men's retreat, this book is just for fun, lacking any social or theological significance.

The Society began by spontaneous combustion. I came to Lake Ellen Camp as interim director in the fall of 1993. On a cold, grey December afternoon I sat alone in the office fighting the deadline for the camp's winter newsletter. A hole on page three leered at me. Gripped by anxiety, I generated a title and let words flow. I never imagined the whimsical Society that nicely filled the offending hole would come to life. But one thing led to another. On Palm

Sunday, 1994, Mike and Arlene Rucinski became the Society's first members by virtue of a $100 bill. Before the year was out, the Society boasted over 100 members and Fort Brainerd on Loon Lake had become reality.

The stories are works of imagination, and any resemblance to persons, places or events past or present is purely intentional.

"God hath chosen the foolish things of the world to confound the wise" (1 Corinthians 1:27).

Lloyd Mattson
The Wordshed
Duluth, Minnesota

Bigfoot

and the
Michigamme Trolls

Background

One November some years ago I was driving toward a forgotten destination when I paused for the night at Lake Ellen Camp. Garry Cropp, camp director and friend, had prepared a room for me in the camp's cozy retreat center. I arrived to find three rigs in the parking area.

Road weary, I headed for my room, but perking coffee and songs bellowing from the fireside room below called for investigation. I found a company of singing deer hunters making preparations for Opening Day on the morrow.

The hunters were Trolls, men who lived below the (Mackinaw) bridge. Seduced by the coffee and song, I joined the company and spent a couple delightful hours swapping stories. Several encounters with these good men in the following years led to the title story of this small book.

A providential circumstance introduced the Trolls to Lake Ellen Camp. One November they arrived in the U.P. for their annual hunt only to find their motel closed and the owner gone with their deposit. A local mentioned a nearby Bible camp that might put them up. Just chance? I don't think so.

The camp director invited the hunters to make Lake Ellen their annual headquarters. After a few visits, the men caught the vision of the camping ministry and began yearly spring treks to engage in work projects, with incalculable benefits to the camp.

I don't recall how it came about, but the men invited me to lead breakfast devotions for the work crew. I looked forward to my annual visits. During my devotional one morning I mentioned the Society and read a story from the archives. I announced my plan to gather archival stories into a small book.

Dick Murphy, one of the original four hunters, hinted that I might want to include some of their hunting adventures in the book. He recounted several stories, but they fell considerably short of the Society's high literary standards. But as I talked with Dick, I sensed he was holding back some dark tale. Patient probing and assiduous research uncovered the Bigfoot story that follows, a tale approaching the probity required for inclusion in the book.

Perhaps you should not attempt to verify the story. Hunters by nature have irregular recall: shot distances, number of points, weight of a buck, etc. Also, after reading the account, you will understand why Dick was loathe to openly acknowledge the Bigfoot legend.

Bigfoot and the Michigamme Trolls

Charles Murphy—Kayo, they call him—eased down on a rotting windfall, his Winchester 270 close by. The moon was about gone and first daylight hinted fog. Not surprising. Nothing was going right this year. Already, he regretted his long underwear.

The weather: that was the first thing to go wrong. Who ever heard of shirt-sleeve weather in the U.P. in November? Sixty degrees opening day, said the radio man. Cooling on the way.

The second thing to go wrong was their territory. Kayo, his sons Dick and Mark and hunting buddy Klaus Zielke had driven 400 miles through the night to scout the Channing Road area where they had hunted for years, only to find a land yacht the size of the Queen Mary parked on their favorite spot. An orange-clad army scurried about stockpiling beer. Not wanting to hunt in the same county with that outfit, Kayo and his partners headed for Lake Ellen Camp where they headquartered, and that's where Darwin Wilson found them.

Darwin was the consummate Yooper, a long-time resident of Michigan's U.P. A faithful volunteer at Lake Ellen Camp, he was famed for his hunting prowess and mostly-true stories. His hunting

9

shack was not far from the camp. Heading home from his shack the evening before Opening Day, he swung through the camp and spotted a van at the retreat center. Guessing it belonged to the Trolls, he hooted his trademark owl hoot and clomped down the stairs to the fireside room. There he found a despondent quartette huddled over a touristy map of Iron County. A coffee pot and German chocolate cake rested nearby.

"Howdy, boys," called Darwin.

"Hi, Darwin," growled Kayo.

Darwin eyeballed the cake. "What's with the map? I thought you boys hunted Channing Road."

Kayo explained about the beer-toting intruders, then grumbled about the unseasonable weather.

Darwin eased a slice of cake from the pan and poured a cup of coffee. "Hunters all over this year. Lots of Trolls. And don't this weather beat all? Happens every 20 years or so. El Nino, I guess. I expect it'll cool tomorrow. Wind due to shift."

"Any suggestions where we might hunt?" asked Kayo.

Darwin wedged in among the map searchers, hmmmd a couple times, and extracted a pencil stub from his shirt pocket. He drew a circle near Hemlock Falls Dam on the Michigamme River a few miles west of the camp. "You might try here. It's real wild country. Should be a few bucks hanging around."

He penciled a route from the camp past Old Mansfield Location to the dam, where he marked an X, "Right here, where the road heads down to the canoe landing, there's an old logging trail heading toward the Michigamme Slough. Rough as a cob, but your rig can handle it. Couple miles in you come to a clearing." He tried another slice of cake. "A hardwood ridge heads northwest with a foot path between it and the river. Maybe a mile up the path you come to an old slashing. Up the ridge you get fair visibility. Post a good shot there and the rest drive. Deer'll head toward the slough right past the post."

Darwin finished his coffee and resisted another slice of cake. "Well, good luck, boys. Don't get lost, it's wild country. And keep an eye out for..." His voice trailed off mysteriously.

Kayo waited, then snapped, "For what?"

Darwin fumbled in his worn wallet and produced a yellowed clipping, which he spread out on the map. The headline said, BIGFOOT SIGHTED ON THE MICHIGAMME.[1]

"Come on, Wilson," snorted Kayo, " you don't believe that stuff!"

"Course not, but those people saw something. Read it. It was close to dark. They didn't stick around to ask questions. And that wasn't the first report of strange things in that country. Like I told you, it's wild." Darwin returned the clipping to his

---

1 For a record of Bigfoot sightings in the Michigamme area, Google Michigan Bigfoot. This quote appears among the entries: "July 1984, Dickenson County, Lake Ellen Baptist Camp on Crystal (sic) Lake: Kids at the camp found a set of three-toed (!) footprints and heard a low growl and later that same night, a scream." The late Darwin Wilson swore he had nothing to do with that.

wallet and clomped up the stairs feeling warm inside. He had fulfilled a Yooper's duty to make Trolls feel right at home.

The hunters wrapped up preparations for the morning and sat around swapping stories of past hunts. Dick, the scholar, launched a Bigfoot lecture. "Legends of mythical creatures abound all over the world. Yeti—the Abominable Snowman, Sasquatch in the Pacific Northwest, Alaskan Natives have their Bigfoot and don't forget the Loch Ness Monster."

Dick was just warming to his subject when Klaus stood up. "Appreciate the information, Dick, but I'm going to bed." Soon the sounds of sleep filled the lodge.

Some time after midnight, Dick sat straight up in bed. "Get away!" he yelled, "Get out of here! Get!" He mumbled something about Bigfoot and resumed snoring.

About four, still half asleep, the hunters climbed in their rig. They followed Darwin's directions along moonlit roads past Old Mansfield Location to Hemlock Dam. It took a while to locate the logging road, and Darwin was right: it was rough! They eased their way to the clearing under the waning moon.

There was no debate who would man the shooting post. Kayo poked about in his duffle bag retrieving a knife, nylon rope, matches sealed in an aspirin bottle, Kleenex, two candy bars, a small water bottle and handful of shells. These he stuffed in the pockets of a faded red hunting coat. The duffel bag held a spare set of clothes. Years of hunting had taught Kayo to prepare for every possibility.

"Give me until good daylight," he said. "Klaus, you take the ridge. Dick, work west of the ridge. Mark, you follow the river." Kayo donned his coat and pulled on a grungy felt hat with a faded red bandana knotted around the crown. He slid five shells in the Winchester then headed up the faint trail.

There's something about opening day. You tune your eyes and ears. You walk quietly, though shooting time may be an hour away. Five minutes up the trail Kayo loosened his coat. Birch, popple, maple and balsam climbed the low ridge to his left. Toward the river, a tangle of dry grass then thick balsam, willow and alder. Even without leaves, brush and thick woods obscured vision. Kayo walked gingerly, stepping over occasional downed trees. Day was beginning to show in the east.

An hour passed, then a serious windfall halted Kayo's progress. Good place for a breather. He cleared sitting space and slipped out of his coat, his rifle within easy reach. Past hunts drifted through his mind. It was great to be in the woods again. The Lord was good!

A breeze stirred and the musky smell of stagnant water filled the morning. Kayo could make out a shallow ditch between the trail and ridge. Black leaves covered the dark water. Then he heard a half-snort, half-whistle not far off. No mistaking that sound! He reached for his Winchester and eased a shell into the chamber, his heart picking up speed. Must be close to shooting time, but no time to quibble.

On the ridge, a small doe minced into view, looking back. Father Whistler wouldn't be far behind. Kayo slipped off the safety. The buck showed, head down, sniffing the ground. Six, maybe eight pointer. Respectable. No matter how long you hunt, the thrill never fades. An open spot ahead. Steady. The Winchester roared. The buck stumbled, got up, stumbled again and leaped from view.

"He won't go far," Kayo assured himself, "That was almost to easy."

Back in the van, three hunters were conserving energy. A distant shot woke them. Dick looked at his watch. "What do you think?"

"Wasn't Dad," Mark said, "Dad never shoots just once." He leaned back to conserve more energy.

But Klaus was full awake. "Soon time to head out, boys. Let's get our stuff together.."

Adrenalin pumping, Kayo grabbed his coat and rifle. The buck should be down, but you never know. It was fair daylight now. He studied the stagnant ditch. Hard to tell how deep. Once he would have jumped it without thought, but those days were long gone. Ahead, a promising log spanned the water, but the promise failed with Kayo's second step. Hurling his rifle forward, Kayo did a respectable half twist, landing flat on his back in stinking muck, his coat and hat flying. Coffee-dark water covered his face and seeped to his long johns. With nothing injured but his pride, he rolled to one knee, retrieved his coat and wrung out his hat. He staggered to dry ground, found his rifle, and sloshed up the ridge thinking unholy thoughts.

Kayo found the deer not 30 yards from where he had shot it, a nice an eight pointer. He dragged it to an open spot and peeled off his foul-smelling shirt, grateful now for the unseasonable warmth. Finding his knife in the sodden coat, he gutted the buck and spread the cavity with a stick.

Wet and miserable, he began to calculate a course of action. Klaus and the boys probably heard the shot, but they wouldn't hurry. Rough terrain would slow them. He had maybe two hours. He worked out of his boots, sox and pants and stood by the deer clad in clammy, stinking long johns. His options did not include simple honesty. He wasn't about to spend the winter listening to stories of Dad falling in the ditch. He would slip unseen to the van, change into his reserve clothes and contrive a story that fell somewhere short of falsehood.

But sneaking a mile through thick brush in sodden clothes was not a pleasant prospect. Old woodsman Kayo conceived a plan. Gathering his clothes, he located a spot in a clump of young balsam. From a coat pocket he dug out the nylon rope and improvised a clothesline between two sturdy saplings and under it built a small fire, grateful for the watertight aspirin bottle. He spread his clothes on the line, using a dry stick for a prop. Steam began to rise.

But the clammy long johns were miserable. Not a soul within miles, his partners two hours away, a warm Indian Summer day dawning. Why not? Kayo added his underwear to the line over the fire, now blazing cheerily. Clad only in boots and a wet felt hat, he observed his handiwork with satisfaction. He hung the wet hat on the clothesline prop.

Gripped by a spirit of adventure, the booted Adam looked about for fuel to speed the drying. He spotted a rotting pine log bristling with dry branch stubs. The stubs pulled loose easily each one ending in a rock-hard, diamond-shaped knot. These he distributed generously on the fire with salutary effect. A steamy cloud rose. You can't beat an old Irishman!

Then Kayo's thoughts turned to the deer. Worthy hunters care for their kill. Upwind and out of sight of his laundry, he cut balsam boughs to shade the deer, an old woodsman trick he had used before. Unfortunately, Kayo's wood lore did not include the BTU potential of pine knots. As he worked over the buck, the fire gathered enthusiasm. The nylon line, no friend of fire, began to sag on both sides of the prop and the laundry followed the sag, concentrating its presence ever closer to the fire. The overtaxed prop snapped, casting the scorched hat a safe distance away, and the Nylon line melted, depositing its burden on the fire, now reaching full vigor. Undeterred by damp garments, the pine knots continued their work. A dark cloud rose

Kayo laid his rifle across the bough-covered buck and stepped back to admire his work. The boys would be proud! Then the cooling breeze caught his attention. As Darwin had predicted, the wind was shifting. Haze filtered the sun and fog began to form. Kayo's primitive condition rendered him decidedly uncomfortable, and he looked forward to the fire and clothes, however damp. He turned toward his laundry, and a plume of dark smoke paralyzed him, but just for a moment. Without regard for life or limb, he ran. Not a square foot of cloth remained.

Fighting panic, Kayo forced himself to think. He counted his assets: a scorched hat, two short lengths of rope from the failed clothesline, a knife, a dead deer, and a rifle. He dismissed the thought of shooting himself. He pondered a furtive mile through the brush in his condition and the possibility that he might not go undetected.

The deer! He could skin the deer, hide the carcass, and make an apron fore and aft. But even if time allowed, it didn't seem prudent to sneak through the woods on Opening Day wearing the hide of a deer. Then Kayo remembered the boughs covering his buck and hope flared.

No pulp cutter could match his speed as he gathered soft balsam boughs. With a rope girdling his waist and chest, Kayo wove a shaggy bough robe worthy of Robinson Crusoe. Beside guarding his modesty, the boughs provided camouflage. Thus clad, a sly woodsman could slip unseen through the forest

The breeze had picked up, chilling the air and the fog thickened as a bough-clad Kayo tugged on his scorched hat and found a walking stick. Leaving his rifle and knife on the buck, he lumbered down the slope toward the trail, skirting the offending ditch. Just as he gained the trail, a fear-tinged voice reached him. "Dad?"

At the van, Klaus checked his watch. "Kayo should be set. We'll poke along and move whatever's in here." He glanced at the sky. "Weather's coming." Dick moved out to drive the western slope of the ridge. Mark fought brush toward the river. Klaus waited for the boys to get in position then made his way to the crest of the ridge.

The pace was slow and noisy, as befits hunters on the drive. An hour passed. No flashing tail. Dick picked up his pace. The terrain led him to guess the slough was not far ahead. As he struggled through the brush up the slope of the ridge, he noting the chilling air and gathering fog. A strange smell reached him. Just as he crested the ridge, something moved. Just for a moment he saw it; a hat, a balsam clump. Something wasn't right. His mouth went dry. "Dad!" Imagination. Too much Bigfoot.

Dick scanned the slope toward the river. Nothing. He came upon the scattered remains of a recent fire. Then he found the deer, knife and rifle. He called again, "Dad!"

Working the ridge, Klaus heard Dick's calls. Fog made the woods almost spooky. He studied the terrain and toward the river. For several minutes he watched and listened. Then he called, "Dick!" Just as he called, he caught movement down by the trail. Whatever it was disappeared, but Klaus had distinct sense of boots, maybe a hat. He lifted his scope for a look, but brush and fog rendered the scope useless. Annoyed by his imagination, He shook himself. He yelled again, "Dick!"

Tangled alder slowed Mark's progress. The woods had turned a misty grey and he concluded no self-respecting buck would hang out in such a place. He angled up toward the trail. As he reached the trail, he heard Klaus call, and hurried to join his companions. As he approached a bend, he heard something, or thought he did. "Klaus?" he called. From the corner of his eye he glimpsed a phantom slipping into the dry grass and balsams toward the river. Mark held his breath, staring, searching. Fog! Imagination. But the image remained of a strange furry creature wearing a hat—like Dad's! Mark picked up his pace until voices drew him up the ridge. He found Dick and Klaus staring down at a gutted deer, and a familiar rifle.

Dick's first frightened call reached Kayo as he shuffled down the ridge toward the trail. He stooped, moving as fast as his costume would allow, grateful for thick brush. No one followed. He grinned. "You boys got to get up early to beat your old dad!" He heard Dick call again.

Hurrying along the trail, Kayo hear Klaus's call and plunged into the balsams toward the river, grateful for his camouflage. Assured by Klaus's second call that he had not been seen, Kayo returned to the trail, confidant that Mark would be out of sight along the river. But at a bend in the trail, there he stood, his eyes fixed on the ridge.

Kayo dived into the dead grass and inched painfully toward the balsams, hardly daring to breath, branch stubs poking his ribs. Surely Mark had seen him. Kayo lay motionless, panting. With detection

19

almost certain, he repented. Conviction gripped his soul. Deception was not right! His sin had found him out. He would give himself up and confess. Then he heard Mark hurrying up the trail and cancelled his repentance.

With the boys a mile away trying to figure things out, Kayo strode quickly to the van and his backup wardrobe. Never did dry clothes feel so good! He returned his forest finery to the woods and did what he could with his soiled skin, but the charred hat would be hard to explain. He was about to yield it to the woods, when an idea struck him. He walked a short distance down the logging road and returned hatless and grinning. Refreshed by dry clothes and the Thermos, Kayo suddenly felt very tired.

Mark, Dick and Klaus stood silently staring at the deer. Mark called, "Dad!" No reply. He turned to Klaus, "You don't suppose he got lost."

"Lost? Not Kayo."

Guardedly, Dick said, "Either of you see anything—unusual?"

"Like what?" asked Klaus sharply.

"1 don't know, just unusual. Animals, anything."

"Too foggy to see much," Mark said. "I gave up on the river. The woods sure change in the fog. You can imagine lots of things. "

Dick looked at him curiously.

Klaus coughed. "Nice buck. Must have been the shot we heard. Kayo probably slipped by us on the trail. Funny he would leave his rifle, though." He grabbed an antler. "Well, let's get back to the van.

I'm sure Kayo will be waiting." But he wasn't at all sure.

Three edgy hunters dragged the buck down to the trail, glancing often into the woods. Kayo heard them coming and walked to meet them. "What kept you boys? I got the buck at sunup. Got too foggy to shoot. Got tired of waiting. Worked my way to the van." He chose his words carefully. "Got sweated up. Changed clothes." That was partly true. "Thanks for dragging in the buck and fetching my rifle. Completely forgot it." That was not true.

The van was still as Kayo guided it along the narrow logging road toward Hemlock Dam. "See anything of Bigfoot?" he asked, just to make conversation. Ahead, just off the trail, a battered felt hat with a soiled red bandana knotted on its crown hung from a broken branch. Every eye saw it. Every eye stared straight ahead. No one said a word.

The Curse of the
Cross-eyed Moose

Introduction

The story first appeared as a serial in the Loon Lake Occasional Newsletter (LLOON), official voice of the Lake Ellen Hunting, Fishing, Camping & Literary Society. Allegedly told at Society meetings by Darwin Wilson, Grand GRUMP (Glorious Royal Unparalleled Majestic Potentate), the story concerns Darwin's distant relative, Wilbur Wilson, who ran a furniture and funeral business in Sagola from the turn of the century into the 40s. The story is set in the early 30s.

Wilbur's Secret Passion

Wilson's Home Furnishings and Funerals
Everything from the Cradle to the Grave.

The sign sprawled across the front of the weathered, two-story frame building on Sagola's main street had been there for so many years folks no longer noticed it. But the neat hand-lettered sign tacked to the front door caught the whole town's attention. Closed. Gone Moose Hunting.

Far as anyone knew, Wilbur Wilson had never hunted anything in his life, not even rabbits. Furthermore, Wilbur never closed the store except Sundays, Christmas Day, Fourth of July and 4-H day at the county fair, where Wilbur judged pickles and his sweetheart, Ella Marie, judged quilts.

Wilbur had courted Ella Marie for 25 years, ever since the Presbyterian box social when Wilber and Ella Marie were 18. The long courtship bothered the

Presbyterian women. When they pressed Wilbur for a wedding date he would reply, "Soon as the business gets on its feet."

At 43, Wilbur stood five-seven, weighed 147 and parted his black gray-flecked hair in the middle. He seldom appeared in public without jacket and tie. TB had taken his mother when he was 13. At 19 Wilber's father sent him to undertaking school in Milwaukee. Wilbur was 37 when his father joined the ranks of the Beloved Departed and Wilbur took over the business.

Like his father, Wilbur was close with a dollar. In spite of this, upon taking over the business, he traded the aging Packard hearse for a late-model Henny funeral coach with white sidewalls and a side-mounted spare, finest coach north of Green Bay. And as his father had done with the Packard and its Model T predecessor, Wilbur appointed the Henny to double as a delivery truck. Some folks found that unsettling.

Aside from the business, Ella Marie was Wilbur's only known passion—if you could call it that. She lived alone in the old family home on the far north edge of town. She had worked in the lumber mill office until the fire. Now she kept books at home for several small businesses. Other than the Presbyterian Church, Ella Maria had little social life.

Slight-built and brown-haired, she was given to bouts of depression. She dreaded large animals, even cows, but kept a lap dog and outdoor dog that slept on the back porch. Neither dog possessed a kindly disposition. Each Sunday Wilbur called and

Ella Marie cooked dinner. Sometimes they went for an afternoon drive, though Ella Marie was not much taken with the hearse.

But Wilbur had another passion. Not a soul knew about it, not even Ella Marie. That passion first stirred when Wilbur was 12 and chanced upon True Hunting Adventures, a forbidden pulp magazine. The cover displayed a terrified lady, dress shockingly torn, fleeing a frothing grizzly. A hunter in jodhpurs and knee-high boots stood nearby, rifle raised. Wilbur sneaked the magazine to his bedroom above the store next to the casket display. He yearned to learn the poor lady's fate and perchance find additional pictures. The lady never appeared again, but Wilbur's search led to a story by the famous outdoor writer, Smokey Camphor.

"Stalking the Deadly Bull Moose" recounted Smokey's moose hunt in the wilds of Ontario. "Pound for pound," wrote Smokey, "the forest knows no more dangerous a beast than a bull moose in rut." Wilbur knew about ruts. His father got dangerous every spring when he drove to Felch Mountain to pick up a Beloved Departed or deliver a couch. You talk about ruts! Wilbur read the story over and over until every scene was etched in his mind. One day, he vowed, he would follow Smokey to Ontario and bag a moose. But he kept that vow to himself.

Wilbur gleaned hunting tips from Field and Stream at Swede Johnson's barbershop. He daydreamed his hunt: the stalk, the dark, menacing form, the clean shot just back of the shoulder. He pictured the stern trophy staring down from above the fireplace in the home he would share with Ella

Marie. Wilbur's vow never waned. Soon as the business got on its feet, he would bag a moose and marry Ella Marie. And now the time had come.

Wilbur Bags a Moose

The packet from Ontario contained a crisp hunting license, moose tag, and hunting regulations in fine print. Early on a crisp October Saturday Wilbur loaded the hearse and drove through Crystal Falls to Iron River, reaching Levinski's Hardware and Sporting Goods just as it opened. He bought ten-inch leather boots, grey wool sox with red tops, a red-and-black checkered wool shirt and gray wool pants, just like Smokey Camphor's. Wilbur chose the biggest sheathe knife in the store. It hung half way to his knee.

Dave Levinski suggested a modified Springfield 30.06 bolt action with a rear sight you could ratchet up for long shots. He added four boxes of shells. "Can't have too many shells; not for moose."

Wilbur headed west on 2, adrenalin flowing. He drove nearly 50! He picked up U.S. 53 east of

Duluth and kept pushing, mile after dusty mile. He reaching Canadian Customs at Fort Francis just before closing time. Assuming the hearse to be on business, the officer tipped his hat and waved Wilbur through.

A few miles into Canada Wilbur found an old gravel pit and pulled in. He made up a bed of furniture pads in the hearse and slept, dog-tired from his 400-mile drive. He awoke at daylight, chilled and stiff. Washing down a cold fried egg sandwich with cold coffee, Wilbur continued north then east, turning north on 105, drawing ever closer to Smokey's hunting territory. The road led through black spruce marsh with willow, aspen, birch, and mountain ash ablaze with red berries.

The town of Chinobish was Sunday quiet when Wilbur pulled in. Across the street a stout, black-haired woman was washing windows at Harold's General Merchandise, Ltd. Wilbur rolled down his window. "Good afternoon, my good woman. Any moose around here?"

The woman put down her bucket and eyed the hearse. "No Moose. But there's Elks in the next town. They meet Thursdays."

"Smart aleck," muttered Wilbur.

"Stupid Yank," grinned the woman.

Just north of Chinobish Wilbur came upon a rutted trail leading west through willow and stunted spruce. Moose country! He recalled Smokey's description. He eased onto the trail, worrying about branches scraping the hearse. The ruts led to an abandoned, overgrown dump. With the sun getting low, Wilbur decided to wait until morning to bag his moose. He found a level spot for the hearse and crawled into his musty bed, but sleep was slow in coming.

Wilbur awoke to an Indian Summer day. He ate another simple breakfast, planning a full dinner after he had bagged his moose. He cut the tags off his new hunting clothes. The wool shirt itched and the boots felt a mite stiff. He threaded his belt through the knife sheathe and slid the 30.06 from its case, trying to recall Dave's instructions.

A little target practice wouldn't hurt. Not wanting to scare off his moose, he aimed the empty rifle at a willow clump. Hold just back of the shoulder. Deep breath. BANG! He whirled and nailed a charging spruce. BANG! BANG! It took a while to figure out how to load the rifle. Then, stuffing a box of shells in his back pocket, he wet a forefinger and lifted it to the breeze. Always hunt into the wind, Smokey had advised. Wilbur plunged into the bush, every pore alert.

Four hours later he was still plunging. His feet were on fire. Sweat trickled down his back. Bagging a moose was taking longer than he figured. Might as well circle back so it won't be so far to drag the critter. Odd, the sun seems to be in the north. Wilbur plunged on, growing anxious. The sun dropped alarmingly low. The rifle weighed a ton. He had no idea he had walked so far from the hearse!

Then he began to hallucinate. He imagined a distant truck grinding through its gears. He slowed his pace to catch his breath. Then, a low, grunting cough stopped him cold. In thick brush, not

20 yards off, loomed a dark form bigger than Eino Maki's Holstein bull. A moose! It's antlers spread at least 30 inches. Wilbur froze. Smokey's words echoed in his head, No more dangerous a beast.

The beast took a step toward him. Around it's neck hung a tattered red apron! The picture flashed through Wilbur's mind: A terrified lady, dress torn, bleeding, defenseless against those cruel horns. He scarcely dared breathe. With neck outstretched and nostrils flared, the moose fixed its terrible eyes on Wilbur. One step, another, another. The moose closed for the kill. Suddenly, Wilbur remembered his rifle. He pumped two shells to the ground before one lodged in the chamber. The 30.06 roared. Again. Again. By chance, the third shot caught the moose in the neck. It reared back, sank to its knees and rolled to the ground, blowing bloody bubbles.

Wilbur grabbed a tree to keep from falling and the hallucinations returned. He imagined a man's voice, "Hey! You all right?" Two very real men approached. One wore a badge, the other a soiled apron." You OK, mister?" said the badge. "We heard your signal..." Then he saw the dead moose. "Why you blathering idiot! You shot Michael!"

"He was charging!" croaked Wilbur. "Those terrible eyes! It was him or me."

"Charging my foot," snorted the policeman, "He was looking for a handout; harmless as a rabbit. Got banged up by the truck that killed his mother. Left him cross-eyed. The town kids raised him from a pup. Named him Michael Moose. We hung that apron on him for fools like you!" The officer eyed Wilbur's knife. "Well, get cracking. If the kids learn about this, I can't guarantee your safety. Where's your rig?"

"Miles from here, by an old dump. I've been looking all afternoon. Where am I?"

"You're not 300 meters from Chinobish. Didn't you hear the traffic? That dump is not a mile up the road. Lucky Harold heard you shoot. Around here, three quick rounds mean trouble. Well, get at that moose. You got a big enough knife."

Trouble was, Wilbur had never dressed anything bigger than a chicken. His voice quavered, "I never shot a moose before. Maybe I could give it to some poor family."

"You think anyone around here would eat Michael? And don't try to sneak off and leave him. I'd love to nail you for wanton waste. Give me your keys. I'll send someone for your rig."

Harold broke in. "I know a couple guys good at dressing game. They'll do it for $15. Bone it, too." Wilbur dared not protest the outrageous price. The men disappeared in the gathering dusk, leaving Wilbur alone, feeling sick.

Soon a stocky young man approached followed by an ancient, weathered dark-skinned man. The old man stared at the moose. "You shoot animal friend? Oh, bum luck! Long time, bum luck. Much bum luck." He lifted his hands and chanted, his voice rising and falling. The young man turned to mask a grin.

"You want the hide?" the old man asked.

"No, just the head. To mount, you know."

The younger man stared at Wilbur. "You're going to stuff Michael?"

The old Indian nudged him with his toe. "Fine trophy. Five dollars more." They set to work with obvious skill.

Near full dark, the officer returned with two husky youths with pack boards. "These boys will pack out the meat. Give 'em a dollar each and they'll keep quiet about Michael until you're out of town." He handed Wilbur his keys. "Why didn't you tell me you drove a hearse? Nearly spooked the kids I sent. They parked it back of Harold's store."

About midnight, Wilbur rolled out of Chinobish with Michael iced down and rolled in oilcloth (another dollar) along one side of the hearse. Primed with coffee and irritable, Wilbur drove through the darkness. No old Indian's curse could scare him! Bum luck? With Roosevelt in the White House, business was picking up. He had bagged his moose, and he would propose to Ella Marie, maybe on Christmas Eve!

The Machete Murder

Wilbur followed the dusty gravel roads toward the border, his 30.06 and knife on the seat beside him. High on coffee, he began talking to Michael. "Got to make the proposal something to remember. Christmas Eve will be perfect. Now, what would be the right gift?" Finally, he pulled off the road and dozed fitfully.

Daylight brought a problem. The business end of the hearse had no ventilation and Indian Summer heat spelled trouble. Michael was sensitive to heat. The border lay just ahead.

Fogged by weariness, Wilbur pulled into U.S. Customs at International Falls. A uniformed man wearing a pistol emerged from the small gray building and eyed the dusty hearse. "What you got in there?"

"Not much. Personal stuff. And Michael. Shot him up near Chinobish."

The man stepped back and unsnapped his holster. "You shot him?"

"Had to. It was him or me."

The customs officer stared at Wilbur. "The Mounties know about this?"

"A policeman helped me load him. Why should the Mounties care? I had a license. Look, mister, I don't have much time. If I don't get ice pretty soon, Michael won't be fit to eat."

The customs officer pulled his gun. "Get out of that rig! Either you're drunk or crazy. Open that back door."

Exasperated, Wilbur stalked to the back of the hearse and jerked open the door. Thin red fluid trickled to the road. The customs man stared at a lumpy, man-sized roll. Keeping an eye on Wilbur, he peeled back the oilcloth. "Meat! Mister, you're sick! Clear out that rig. No telling what you're trying to sneak across the border."

Wilbur hurled his gear to the drive and the customs officer probed it with his toe. "OK. Now get out of here, and don't ever try a stunt like that again!"

A dust cloud followed Wilbur down the road. He drove hard, praying for ice. Two hours; nothing. But as he entered the town of Cook, his spirits soared. A tall sign with a red star. Homer's Texaco. Gas, Bait, Ice. Wilbur pulled up to the gravity-flow pump, slipped his knife from its sheath to chip ice, and entered the station.

He found Homer tilted back in a ratty chair behind a cluttered desk absorbed in the Mesabi Daily

News. The headline, hidden from Wilbur's eyes, read, MACHETE MURDERER HUNTED. The story concerned an old lumberjack who had been hacked to death in his cabin. The News called it the Machete Murder. Wilbur waited a minute than barked, "Fill 'er up. Where's your ice?"

Startled, Homer looked up to see a red-eyed, unshaven man wearing soiled clothes, a long knife in his hand. Through the open door he saw a dusty, black hearse. He nearly fell off his chair. "I'll get your gas, Sir," he croaked, "Ice is out back."

Wilbur hurried out the back door and Homer approached the hearse but never pumped gas. In the gloom of the hearse he saw a headless corpse wrapped in oilcloth. On the front seat lay a rifle. Homer stumbled across the road and ran a half block south to Irma's Coffee Pot. He collapsed on a stool. "He's here! Call the sheriff!"

Not given to hysteria, Irma shoved a glass of water across the counter. "Calm down, Homer. Who's here?"

"The Machete Murderer! He's got a huge knife. He stole a hearse. There's a body in it with no head!"

Irma stepped to the door. Sure enough, a shabby man stood at the back of a hearse at Homer's station. Irma cranked the wall phone furiously and waited. "Maybelle, where you been? Find the deputy real quick. The Machete Murderer's at Homer's station!" She glanced out the window. "Lord, Help us!" The dusty hearse moved slowly by.

When Wilbur returned with a block of ice, Homer was nowhere in sight. Disgusted, he laid the ice next to Michael and tossed a quarter on Homer's desk. Hang the gas. He had enough to get to Virginia. He drove slowly south, bent on finding a spot to ice down Michael and take a breather. He came to a sandy trail leading through a stand of jack pine. Wilbur followed the trail to a clear spot, chipped ice over Michael, then stretched out on the warm brown grass and pine needles. Michael was safe. Ella Marie was waiting. Life was good. Hang the old Indian! He fell into a delicious sleep.

It took Maybelle a while to locate the deputy and a while for the deputy to reach the Coffee Pot. He quizzed Homer briefly then phoned the State Troopers in Virginia. He identified himself. "Homer, runs the Texaco station in Cook, swears he saw the Machete Murderer. He's got a big knife and a rifle; driving a stolen hearse. Homer says he saw a body in it. Irma saw the hearse heading south. Fifteen, twenty minutes ago. How about a road block at Old 169?" The deputy took off, siren howling.

The siren ended Wilbur's nap. Accident, he muttered. He stretched and climbed into the hearse. He headed down 53, delighted by a burst of inspiration. "Of course! What a great gift for a young lady!"

He was rehearsing his proposal when flashing red lights in the distance interrupted his thoughts. Must be a bad accident. As he drew nearer, he saw a steel-wheeled tractor and farm wagon sprawled across the road flanked by Trooper cars. Then Wilbur saw guns. "A roadblock! They must be after a crook!"

He skidded to a stop fifty yards short of the roadblock and slid across the seat and out the passenger door, grabbing his 30.06, forgetting it wasn't loaded. He crouched by the front fender, his heart pounding. A trooper shouted something and a discomforting thought crossed Wilbur's mind. The crook could be anywhere, even behind him! He rose to one knee to look around and a shot echoed through the woods. Losing all enthusiasm for police work, Wilbur rolled under the hearse.

Feet slowly approached. "Throw out that rifle!" commanded the feet. *They got him!* thought Wilbur and he began crawling out, shoving the 30.06 before him. The trooper slammed his foot on the rifle and pointed a revolver at Wilbur's head. "Don't move!"

Wilbur saw a uniformed man open the back door of the hearse. "Meat!" he howled, "Nothing but bloody meat, and a bloody moose head!"

Wilbur was flabbergasted. "It's a crime to haul moose meat through Minnesota? I thought you were after a crook. I was only trying to help."

The trooper lifted Wilbur to his feet and checked his driver's license, noting his Michigan address matched the plates on the hearse. "Our apologies, Mr. Wilson. I take it you don't know about the Machete Murder?" The trooper explained. "You scared the liver out of Homer!" he said.

The trembling would not stop as Wilbur drove toward Duluth. The old Indian's curse, the man at

Customs, Homer, then I nearly get shot. He shouted back toward Michael. "You're nothing but trouble. I should dump you in the brush right now. You already cost me a fortune." Wilbur drove on, still trembling. He didn't believe in curses.

The Curse Strikes Again

The shoot-out made Wilbur wonder, but the rest of the trip went fine. A cold front arrived east of Duluth, so Michael was safe. The hearse hummed along. A plan for Ella Marie's Christmas Eve surprise slowly evolved, stirring Wilbur's blood. "Wilbur, you sly old fox, this is one Christmas Ella Marie will never forget." He had no idea how right he was.

Sagola was frost-covered and asleep when Wilbur eased the hearse into the old shed behind the store. He stumbled up the stairs to his living quarters and fell into bed. Just before dawn he awoke in a cold sweat. His bed was rolling down US 2. The old Indian stood over him, swaying and moaning.

Wilbur buried his head under the pillow and slept until noon.

While he soaked in the claw-footed tub, he plotted the afternoon. He would deliver the meat to Father Winofski, who looked after several poor families. Next, he would phone the taxidermist in Marquette. In the evening he would visit Ella Marie and tell her to expect a Christmas Eve surprise.

Father Winofski was less than enthused about moose meat of doubtful vintage, but he accepted it. The taxidermist was another matter. Wilbur tried to barter for a funeral then offered a generous discount on furniture. But the taxidermist wanted cash, lots of cash. Wilbur slammed down the phone.

Then he remembered Hank Johnson from Johnson Junction, a handyman he occasionally hired. He recalled Hank was working on a correspondence course with Northwestern School of Taxidermy, whose magazine ads promised success or your money back. Wilber phoned Johnson Junction and the operator tracked down Hank.

"Hank? Wilbur Wilson. Fine. Business is good. Say, I just got back from a moose hunt in Canada. How are you coming with that taxidermy business?"

Hank reported he had stuffed a red squirrel and the neighbor's cat that got run over in a hay field and they turned out real good. Next lesson was about deer heads. Hank neglected to mention that the deer head lesson was waiting on another payment.

"You're just the man I'm looking for," said Wilbur. "I got a job for you, if you think you can handle it. But you must keep it a secret."

Early the next morning Wilber slipped out of town with Michael's salted-down head wrapped in burlap and stuffed in a furniture crate. He found Hank in a small, foul-smelling shed. He explained his need. "Take your time and do a good job. I'll cover expenses and give you $25, $10 down. But I must have the head before Christmas Eve, and you mustn't tell a soul, or the deal is off."

Twenty-five dollars was more money than Hank had ever possessed in his life. He agreed to tackle the job and sent right off for the deer head lesson. But what with grouse hunting and deer hunting and Hank's total ignorance of head mounting, the job dragged on. The deer head lesson proved tougher than Hank expected and finding supplies was not easy. October faded and November dragged into December.

Wilbur began to worry. He phoned Johnson Junction. "Everything's just fine," Hank said. "You'll have your moose in plenty of time." But Hank was overly optimistic. He was good to figure things out, but the lesson called for a form and that posed a problem. Then he recalled a large, moldy buck with a broken antler gathering dust in the back room at Ben Johnson's Feed Store. He borrowed it. The eyes would come in handy too. Not one person in a thousand could tell the difference between deer eyes and moose eyes. He hung a moose picture in his shop for a model and set to work, and Michael began to look quite respectable.

Three days before Christmas, Michael was complete, except for the eyes. The correspondence course called for a cement Hank had never heard of. He invented a thick glue from flour, water, saw-dust and a dash of Portland cement. He carefully pressed the eyes in place, rotating them just right. He stepped back to admire his work then phoned a panicking Wilbur. It was December 23.

Elated, Wilbur headed for Johnson Junction. In the dim light of Hank's shop Michael looked impres-sive. Ella Marie was one lucky girl! He gave Hank a five dollar bonus.

"Be careful," Hank warned, "Them eyes ain't quite set. Won't be firm until morning."

Wilbur drove cautiously and slowly, planning to arrive home late. He backed the hearse to the work-room door where he admitted the Beloved Departed. With great care he lugged Michael inside, alarmed at how heavy he was. He placed him gently on the floor and leaned him back against a table in the mortuary workroom. Michael was one handsome animal! Wilber went to bed, his heart aglow. What curse?

Satan, Wilbur's black tomcat, was a first-class mouser that roamed freely through the building. About midnight, lured by a strange smell, he en-tered the mortuary storeroom and came face to face with a hairy monster. Fur rose on Satan's back, his tail bristled. He hissed and swiped a paw at the intruder, causing Michael to rock ever so slightly. Taking that as aggression, Satan leaped, tangling his claws on Michael's extended nose. He pitched forward, landing hard and tilting awkwardly. Satan yowled and fled in terror.

The yowl failed to reach Wilbur. He slept peacefully and awoke refreshed. It was the day before Christmas. He had decided not to open the store, but spend the day preparing for the most exciting evening of his life. He would hang a balsam garland with a red heart around Michael's neck. He would present it to Ella Marie and then he would propose. Contrary to Ella Marie's teetotaling scruples, Wilbur bought an bottle of expensive wine.

When Wilbur entered the store room, panic ripped away his light spirit. Michael leaned awkwardly on his nose and an antler. He eased the head upright and stared in shock. Michael's right eye glared fiercely down his nose; his left eye turned upward, as though in prayer. Hank's cement had set rock hard. Cross-eyed in life, Michael was cross-eyed in death! Though his gift was disfigured, there was nothing to do but pursue the plan. Repairs would come later. Ella Marie would understand.

The Christmas Eve Surprise

Snow began to fall as Wilbur fixed the balsam garland around Michael's neck and loaded him into the hearse. Michael was heavy! Sagola's faithful were in church and the streets were deserted as Wilbur drove to Ella Marie's. On the way, he rehearsed each step. Ella Marie was expecting him. He would approach her door silently with Michael. She would answer his knock. He would shout Merry Christmas! and present his gift, the trophy of a lifelong dream. Then he would sweep Ella Marie into his arms, kiss her, and propose. Wilbur's eyes misted.

To enhance the surprise, Wilbur parked well back from the house. Snow fell harder as he eased Michael from the hearse. The only way he could carry his trophy any distance was to approach from the back, wrap his arms around the neck and lean backward. But this obscured Wilbur's vision, a factor he had not considered.

One small bulb lit the walk to Ella Marie's porch, where ancient cedars crowded the three steps up to the door. The living room light was on. Wilbur's heart quickened. Ella Marie was waiting! What he did not know was that his bride-to-be sat glued to her Philco, absorbed in The Christmas Carol, her little dog in her lap. Old Marley's ghost groaned and rattled his chain as Wilbur struggled up the walk.

Then, a complication: Michael completely filled the space between the snow-clad cedars, hiding the steps and blocking access to the door. There was no way Wilbur could knock without setting Michael down, and that would ruin the surprise. With strength fading, he reverted to a practice from childhood. He called out, Oh Ella Marieeee!

His call blended with dead Marley's wail and Ella Marie jumped. The little dog bristled. The outside dog forsook his bed and set out to investigate. And Wilbur's plan fell apart. As a frightened Ella Marie opened the door, her little dog swept past and fastened on Wilbur's ankle, just as the outdoor dog clamped onto Wilbur's backside, driving him involuntarily forward. From the snowy darkness a furry monster with terrible eyes lunged for Ella Marie. She screamed and fainted. The neighbor's porch light came on.

Panic drove Wilbur across the yard dragging Michael, the dogs in pursuit. He stumbled through knee-deep snow to the balsam woods behind Ella

Marie's house. Shaking and gasping, he threw the accursed moose in a tangle of brush and staggered to the hearse. He drove off without lights, but not before anxious neighbors caught a glimpse of the familiar vehicle.

The neighbors found Ella Marie unhurt but out cold. They summoned Doctor Phipps, who had often treated Ella Marie's depression. Gently, he brought her back to awareness and listened as she sobbed out an improbable story. "There, there," said the good doctor, "It's quite common to have emotional stress during holidays. You're going to be fine, but you need rest." He phoned the mental hospital at Newberry.

Things turned bad for Wilbur after Christmas. He was sick about Ella Marie and stories flew about town. How could he explain? He had told not a soul about his Christmas surprise. In retrospect, the whole plan seemed silly. And Hank, his only witness, had left for a CCC camp somewhere in Minnesota. Worse, Michael had disappeared!

At first light the day after Christmas Wilbur had gone to the balsam woods intending to dispose of the accursed animal forever. Michael had to be right here, but he wasn't. Michael wasn't anywhere. Had the curse spirited him away?

Indeed, Michael had been spirited away, but not by the curse, but by two brothers from Sagola. They had gone rabbit hunting on Christmas day with their new .22 and stumbled upon a strange, snow-covered lump in the balsam woods. The lump turned out to be a ratty moose head with strange yes. Figuring an amateur taxidermist's had cast off his failure, the boys appropriated Michael for their hunting shack over by Ralph, a shack they shared with three cousins from Felch Mountain. Parents being what they are, the boys thought it best not to report their find.

Wilbur finally gained permission to visit Ella Marie at the Newberry mental hospital. A kindly nurse guided him to her room and stood by. He found Ella Marie pale and frightened. Taking her hand, he told her how he much missed her. He told her about his hunt and Michael and Hank and the accident that made Michael look so fierce. He did not mention the curse or his plan to propose.

Ella Marie looked puzzled and began to cry. The nurse led Wilbur away. "It is nice of you to care," she said, "but please don't reinforce her hallucinations with strange tales. She will recover in time."

And it would take time.

The Felch Mountain Baptist Pot Luck

The Sagola brothers who kidnapped Michael were Catholic, and that concerned the Felch Mountain Ladies Missionary Society, for the Sagola brothers spent a lot of time with their three Felch cousins, who were Baptist. The Missionary Society frowned on Baptist boys consorting with Catholics. Back in those days, church folks could get a mite touchy.

Take August MacDougal. August hailed from Inverness-shire on Loch Ness in the Scottish Highlands. He had bought a farm and on a small lake west of Sagola and named it Loch Ness Farm. The lake wasn't much; a few hundred acres, bass and bluegills, now and then a northern. The farm stretched along a narrow bay formed by a wooded point that ended in a reedy sand bar. August mowed the slope to the bay, providing a fine spot for picnics and swimming. The Sagola brothers and their Baptist cousins regularly borrowed his boat to fish and explore the lake.

August was staunch, devout Presbyterian. One Sunday he took issue with the sermon. The debate gathered steam and August stalked from the church vowing never to return. Staunch man that he was, he kept his word.

It happened that the eldest MacDougal son was courting a Swede-Finn girl from the Felch Mountain Baptist Church. Soon the whole MacDougal clan began worshiping with the Baptists, though August eschewed the Baptist's abundant waters of baptism.

Forsaking the Presbyterians did not weaken August's loyalty to Scotland and Calvinism, and as spring approached, a circumstance arose that convinced him his church relocation had been pre-destined. Each July the Ladies Missionary Society held week-long missions festival that began with a Sunday rally day climaxed with a Saturday picnic. Guest speaker for the upcoming festival would be a Dr. Robert MacLeod, veteran missionary to Darkest Africa and noted pulpiteer. Like August, Dr. Mac-Leod hailed from the shores of Loch Ness in Scotland. August immediately offered to host the good doctor, and he invited the ladies to hold their picnic at Loch Ness Farm.

As the festival approached, by unfortunate co-incidence, the Iron Mountain Daily News ran a story about an alleged recent sighting of the Loch Ness

Monster. This fueled enthusiasm throughout the area for the notable Scottish preacher's visit.

The capacity crowd that filled the church on Rally Day included Lutherans, Presbyterians and sprinkling of Catholics, including the Sagola brothers. By tradition, a potluck followed the morning service, at which time the guest speaker would answer missionary questions. Dr. MacLeod was a down right hit. Tall and genial with fuzzy white sideburns, he spoke with a delightful burr preserved through 40 years in Africa and America. He preached a powerful sermon. The offering set a record.

But things fell apart at the potluck. Rather than questions about Darkest Africa, the children bombarded Dr. MacLeod with queries about the Loch Ness Monster. "Did you ever see the monster?" asked a small boy.

"Well, laddie, in a manner of speakin'. From the hills above the loch, we boys would sometimes see a dark shadow moving in the water and strange ripples, when therrre was no wind. Oh, we were surrre Nessie was therrre! And at night—the moanin!" August MacDougal snickered.

"Is the monster dangerous?" asked a wide-eyed girl.

Dr. MacLeod gripped the arms of his chair. "Therrre's many and many a tale, me lassie. Sheep in the meadow, gone without a trace. Once, a calf. And one dearrr old woman, out looking for her coos, she niver came home!" Dr. MacLeod wiped a tear.

"Could monsters live in our lakes?" the girl asked.

"Ah, lassie, who knows? Therrre are mysteries beyond knowing in the Crrreator's great wirld. Pray the dear Lord everrry day to keep you safe!"

The Missionary Society president coughed and closed the meeting, and three Baptist boys, in the grip of total depravity, slipped away with their Catholic cousins. Soon a rusting Model A was wending its way toward the hunting shack near Ralph.

Farewell to the Cross-eyed Moose

Dr. MacLeod's wit and charm drew women from several churches to Loch Ness Farm for the missionary picnic. Ella Marie, pale and quiet, was among the Presbyterian ladies—her first venture into society since her hospital stay. Three men were present: August MacDougal, Dr. MacLeod and Wilbur, his hearse parked discretely behind the barn. He was startled to see Ella Marie. He smiled. She nodded, coolly.

Dr. MacLeod was in rare form. He bowed and beamed, chucked babies and occasionally forgot his burr. An improvised plank table covered with blue-and-white checkered oilcloth displayed Swedish meatballs, pickled herring, cinnamon-brown rice pudding, escalloped potatoes with ham, fried chicken, varieties of baked beans, sparkling cucumber pickles, Svenska limpa buns, deep red Jell-O heaped with melting whipped cream, cookies, cakes and pies.

Warm hazy skies greeted the picnickers, but as the children romped and women visited, awaiting the feast, clouds began to gather. Thunder murmured. The Society ladies grew nervous. The missionary message and offering were more important than eating.

Blankets spread on the sloping lawn served younger women with children. A double half-circle of wooden folding chairs accommodated older women. With his back to the lake, Dr. MacLeod launched into his address. His deep voice—burr restored—described the evils that stalked impoverished Darkest Africa. "Oh, for people to grieve! For people to go! For people to give, give, give!" The Society treasurer glowed.

Then, in his darkest, deepest voice, "Ah, Africa indeed is dark, but what perils lurk in this our land? Perhaps in this very community?"

The ladies sat spellbound, hushed. Then they froze. From the wooded point across the narrow bay came a low moaning that swelled to a shriek. An apparition arose, Half-hidden by reeds, a fearsome horned creature with a long, undulating body that rose and fell with the moaning. A child cried. A woman screamed. Dr. MacLeod turned and blanched. "Good Lord!" he cried. Wilbur stared in disbelief, the old Indian's chant echoing in his head.

Then the apparition disappeared, but the picnic was over. Women dashed for the cars, dragging

their children. August went for his shotgun. Dr. MacLeod, pale and shaken, knelt in prayer.

On the far side of the wooded point five wet boys watched bubbles rise from a creature they had buried at sea. Bundling a soaked drop cloth borrowed from Sagola Painting and Decorating, the boys scrambled into a rusting Model A and bounced across the field toward the road that led to Ralph.

Wilbur found Ella Marie staring toward the wooded point, forgotten in their haste by her Presbyterian friends. Wilbur walked quietly to her and slipped his arm around her waist.

"Your moose?" she said.

Wilbur nodded.

"How?"

Wilbur spread his hands.

Ella Marie smiled, then giggled, then she hugged Wilbur, and hand in hand they walked to the hearse that waited behind the barn.

Evolution and Grandma Hoppola's Fine Jersey Cow

Introduction

Allegedly by Jim Carpenedo

Jim and Shirley Carpenedo live with their two lovely, lively daughters on the Black River just north of Bessemer, Michigan. One summer evening I stopped by and taught Jim to fly fish. He took a trout and I did not. I did not fish with him again.

As you will note in the story, Jim became a fishing addict, neglecting his family and despoiling his character.

The Carpenedos showed up at the first Society Hip Boot Award banquet, at which time members submitted entries to the annual literary contest. Jim's entry came as something of a surprise, for he was not known for literary skills, which his entry confirms. But since his was the sole entry, the story had to be considered.

Shy and retiring, Jim asked the Scribe to read his story. The audience listened in stunned silence. The judges scribbled furiously (see concluding note). The story did show a certain flair, and without competition, Jim was awarded the coveted Hip Boot.

Evolution and Grandma Hoppola's Fine Jersey Cow

At first, I was never going to tell a soul what happened at Grandma Hoppola's pool, but then I figured I owed it to science, so here goes:

As you know, there's fair trout in the Black and I've caught my share since an old geezer stopped by one evening and taught me to fly fish. I'm not a purist, you understand. Feed 'em what they're eatin', that's my motto. But nothing in all my fishing years could have prepared me for that Thursday night at Grandma Hoppola's pool.

I got home from work about six and the air felt just right. Trout fishermen will understand. Shirley mumbled something about supper, but being an understanding wife, she tossed a tuna sandwich and three oatmeal cookies in my lunch bucket along with a jar of cold milk. I pecked her on the cheek and headed for the river, pausing at the worm box for a handful of crawlers, which I tossed in the lunch bucket some distance from the cookies. Fixing to bank fish, I left my boots and landing net behind.

Grandma Hoppola lives across the river from our place, about a quarter-mile downstream. She is as sweet a little old lady as you ever met. She keeps a useless black dog, several cats and a fine Jersey cow named Posy, a real good milker.

Just below Grandma's place the river forms a respectable pool—four, five feet deep in places. At the head of the pool there's a long, grassy island with weeds drooping over the water. The riff past the island makes a great place to lay a fly and let it drift natural like into the pool.

I reached the river with good light left and laid a Caddis on the riff. Three, four more casts produced nothing so I worked downriver, side casting to drift the far bank. I fished maybe a half hour then decided to soak a crawler whilst I ate my sandwich.

I headed back to the head of the pool and sat down, leaning against a popple. When I opened my lunch bucket, don't you suppose the milk had leaked? The sandwich and cookies were a total loss, but the worms were happy as clams at high tide, fat with milk. Disgusted, I looped a fat crawler on the Caddis and swung it into the pool, expecting nothing. I propped the rod between my legs and leaned back.

I guess I nodded off. Then a bump on the rod got my attention. Easing to one knee, I watched the line ease upstream. Red horse, I figured. Gathering slack, I set the hook. Whoa! That was one big sucker! The fish ripped upstream, and when it broke water, I near fainted. I had a hold of the mother of all trout!

Up and down the pool she tore, leaping, sounding, sulking. All I could do was hang on. It was close to dark before the fish gave up and let me slide it onto the grass at the head of the pool. I was shaking so bad I could hardly stand. At my feet lay the biggest trout the Black ever saw—over 30 inches, and fat! Maybe 15 pounds!

Sportsman that I am, I pondered what to do. Such a fish deserves to live, but if I turned her loose, who would believe me? On the other hand, if I hung her on the wall, every time I saw that fish I'd get proud and Shirley is dead set against pride. I might even hook a fly in her jaw, which would be close to a lie. Shirley is against lying too.

Finally I made up my mind and reached for the trout, but when I touched her she gave a mighty flop and landed four feet out in the pool. I made it only three. I slogged home through the dark, chilled and disgusted.

When I walked in the door, Shirley laughed and laughed. I knew it was no time to tell her about the fish. I hit the shower and went to bed, but sleep was slow coming.

You can bet I hit the river the next evening, taking my boots and net. I worked crawlers until dusk, using every trick known to man, but not a nibble. I was about to give up when I heard a mamma mallard quacking downriver with a troop of yellow ducklings. They was so cute! They bounced down the riff and floated calmly into the pool.

Suddenly, Wham! Plop! Wham! Mama squawked furiously and took off, but those poor little fellers—they peeped pitifully and paddled hard as they could, but one by one they got et up. Now I knew muskies et ducklings. Northerns will too. But trout? Then I remembered the big one that got away. Something mighty strange was going on in the Black.

Then I heard Posy's gentle bell. Grandma came down the trail with her fine Jersey cow. I called softly so's not to scare her, "Evenin', Grandma."

"Oh! That you, Jim? How's fishin'?"

"Poor," I replied. I waded across for a visit. I could see right off that Grandma was troubled.

"Something's bad wrong, Jim. Evenings, Posey's fine, but mornings, she gives hardly any milk and barely eats. Something else. Used to be, I'd call her and she'd come right away. Now I have to fetch her from the river. What do you suppose ails her?"

I watched Posy. She stood belly deep in the pool, facing upstream, as though she was waiting for something. She sure didn't look sick.

"It's a worry, Jim," said Grandma. She loved her little cow.

We chatted a while, then Grandma called, "Come, Posy." Reluctantly, the little Jersey left the pool and followed Grandma up the dark path, and I turned loose my scientific brain. It was a puzzler for sure. I decided to investigate.

I hit the pool by first light Saturday and soon I heard Posy's bell. She waded in and faced upstream, her eyes seemed fixed on the grassy island at the head of the pool. Soon a clump of juicy weeds broke loose and drifted toward Posy. She stretched out her neck, wrapped her tongue around the weeds, and commenced to chew.

"Aha!" I said.

Another weed chunk drifted down and Posy captured it. That was one smart cow. She had found the exact spot where weeds would drift by. No wonder she was off her feed mornings. About then the sun poked above the trees, giving me a better look, and what I saw blew my mind.

In the riff close to the island, two huge fish fanned the current, poking their snouts into the overhanging weeds. They worried a chunk loose and it drifted toward Posy. Then another chunk. I was stunned. The trout were feeding the cow!

But what came next really staggered me. Just under the surface near Posy's hindquarters I saw

two dark forms. A milky wisp drifted down the pool. The fish lay motionless. They were feeding off Posy!

Now I knew about milk snakes. A professor explain them to me one morning up river. It seems a Holstein wandered into a marsh near Hayward, where a bunch of bull snakes was frog hunting. A nearsighted snake latched onto the Holstein by mistake and got a pleasant surprise. In no time, other snakes caught on and in two or three weeks milk snakes got to be a regular thing. "That's how evolution works," said the professor. I never actually saw a milk snake, but you got to believe a professor.

And there stood Posy, calm as a queen, packing in juicy weeds, while two, sometimes three trout fed. Symbiosis, I think the professor called it. I was seeing evolution unfold before my very eyes!

Scientific questions whirled in my brain. How did Posy learn where to stand? How did trout learn that Posy liked weeds, and how did they know Posy gave milk? Or how to get at it? You just got to leave such stuff to professors.

I kept watching. After while, the weeders drifted down to Posy and the drinkers moved to the weeds. Like bees and ants, the trout were organized. It all came together. I understood why that milk-fat crawler attracted my giant trout and how Black River trout got big enough to eat ducklings.

Then I heard Grandma coming. "Soooo, bossy, bossy. Come Posey." I slipped out of sight. Posy stirred and the trout flashed away and the little cow splashed out of the pool and followed Grandma up the trail.

I hiked home, my head awhirl. What to do? I could hardly tell Shirley or Grandma. Women can't handle scientific stuff. Finally I picked up the phone. "Hey, Grandma. Jim here. I've been thinking. Must be something in the river got Posy's system upset. How about I come over and gate off the trail so she can't wander down to the river any old time?" And that's what I did.

The next Saturday Grandma came over with an apple pie and jar of wild raspberry jelly. Posy was her old self again, she said, feeding good mornings and giving lots of milk. "But I tell you, Jim, Posey sure hates that gate you built!"

Grandma hugged me and Shirley patted me on the head and said I was so smart. I guess I am smart, about scientific things, anyhow. I'm sure glad I threw back that big trout. It would never do to be both proud and smart.

Editor's note

The judges' review of the Carpenedo story revealed two flaws that threatened its approval. First, the evolution of the milk snakes from frog basic eaters took several years, not "two or three weeks," as Carpenedo asserts. But the alleged milk fish phenomenon proved more troublesome.

Then the research staff turned up a scholarly anthology, The One that Got Away (Greenberg and Waugh, editors; Bonanza Books, New York, 1989). On page 154 Eugene E. Slocum recounts the experience of a clergyman on a stream in Hopkins's pasture. The minister clearly observed the milk fish phenomenon. The incident involved a heifer and a German brown trout. Weed feeding, however, was not observed. This could be attributed to [1. a more primitive stage of evolution; [2. lower intelligence among German brown trout (Salmo trutta), or [3. The frustration any trout would experience trying to extract milk from a heifer. Satisfied, the judges awarded Carpenedo his prize, which hangs today over his fireplace.

The Ablution of Tim McGreen

Introduction

The following story in verse concerns a dues-paying member of the Minnesota Chapter of the Lake Ellen Hunting, Fishing, Camping & Literary Society. Modesty prevents identifying the poem's creator, who falls just short of blatant plagiarism.

Tim Green is the youngest member of the Green family. For 17 years the late Roger Green and his wife Lois along with sons Doug and Tim commuted from Duluth to Alaska to mine gold.

Tim gained notoriety in Fairbanks for his remarkable gift of grime. Mothers would remove small children from the sidewalk when Tim passed by. One person said, "If Tim walks within three feet of a grease bucket, the grease will leap out and grab him." Knowing he would soon get soiled again, Tim concluded it was a waste of time to clean up. Hence, the legend. The story first appeared at a reception as the Greens returned home from their summer venture.

Tim has since married a lovely girl named Connie and has become quite respectable. Tim and Connie and their three boys divide their time between Fairbanks and their winter home near Cook, Minnesota, a town you encounter in "The Curse of the Cross-eyed Moose."

The Ablution of Tim McGreen

With a nod to the shade of the Bard of the North

We've heard oft times of Sam McGee
And Dangerous Dan McGrew,
Tales long old from the land of gold,
Tales the sourdoughs knew.
But of all strange sights under northern lights,
The most fearful ever seen,
Was that terrible week on Dynamite Creek,
When they captured Tim McGreen.

Some say McGreen was not as mean
As legend would declare.
He was tall and thin with a boyish grin,
And D8 grease in his hair.
He first came north to venture forth
To a gold claim up the Steese.
'Twas Tim's dread of a bath
That stirred men's wrath,
And shattered the Arctic peace.

In the cool of spring it was no big thing,
As zephyrs blew from the South,
But by Midnight Sun and the salmon run,
It was known to the Yukon's mouth.
While summer slept a foul breeze swept,
Wilting the tundra flowers.

Like salmon dead in the river bed,
Awaiting the cleansing showers.
A trooper, they say, up Fairbanks way
Issued the first release.
Something's real bad, like a grizzly gone mad,
Killing up on the Steese.
Mountain ewe and caribou
Fled to distant hills.
Ptarmigan, goose, bear and moose,
All sought far Arctic chills.
A Ruby man aboard his skiff
Sniffed the southbound air.
In alarm he swore, as he rushed ashore,
"Something's bad dead up there!"

Grayling died in the murky tide
Washed down from Tim's far claim.
The Sierra Club in a Dawson Pub
Decried McGreen's foul shame.
Nor man nor beast could stand the least
Of this strange man's pollution.
Clear up the Slope the only hope
Was Tim McGreen's ablution.

But who would dare to risk the air
Where this strange man was mining?
Alaska's best, put to the test,
Refused, discretely declining.
Ten Indians, six Aleuts, and one Eskimo
Boldly weighed the cost.
They made their choice and raised their voice:
"We go, or all is lost!"

They made their way to a hill one day,
And scanned the scene to the west.
There lay McGreen, lithe and lean,
Taking his evening rest.
Boots and sox strewn on the rocks,
His Carhartts wore a dark glaze.
No insect dared what skin was bared,
There arose a sullen haze.

Aha! said the spies, as they fixed their eyes
On the resting form below,
We take him when his sleep grows deep,
We hope the east winds blow!
Through the endless light of the summer night
They prayed they might prevail,
For man and beast along the Steese
Were doomed if they should fail.

In the morning chill, when all was still,
At dawning of the day,
With stealthy glide from the upwind side,
The men crept toward their prey.
And Indian fell beneath the smell,
The rest pursued their way.
Then their gaze met a cargo net
That would hold a beluga whale.
Thy grasped its strands with trembling hands
And stole across the shale.

With one great leap they broke Tim's sleep
And bound him in their wrath.
"McGreen," they cried, as the Eskimo died,
"This day you take a bath!"

Tim yelled and fought, the net held taut,
An Aleut fired up the Cat.
The mountains rang as the winch line sang,
And Tim removed his hat.

Slow, ever slow, to the pool below
The D8 dragged its prey.
The waters deep began to sweep
The vapors from the day.
A dark film rose from Tim's worn clothes
And drifted down the race.
A strange look spread, a look of dread,
Across McGreen's wet face.
He stood upright in the morning light
And the stream began to clear.
McGreen bent down then formed a frown,
His young face lost its fear.
Then he shot a grin at the pallid skin
Mirrored back from the clearing pool,
"Well, howdy Buck, and lots of luck,
I ain't seen you since school!
Since I left home the North to roam,
To seek this life serene,
I declare, by foul or fair,
It's the first time I've been clean!"

So the legend's told when nights are cold
And northern lights are seen,
Of that dread week on Dynamite Creek,
When they abluted Tim McGreen.

Epilogue

Life is the sum of its friends and memories. You learn that as the years come on and values fall in place. My richest memories and deepest friendships relate to camping and the outdoors. No matter where life took me these 80-plus years, I got involved one way or another in the outdoors and camping.

I cannot account for this. I was born with a love for the creation, and one day in my youth I met the Creator, at a camp.

The Society and Fort Brainerd grew largely out of conversations with the late Darwin Wilson, outdoorsman and long-time friend. He stopped by often during my brief tenure as Lake Ellen's interim director. While he bears no blame for dreaming up the Society, he came on board with enthusiasm and was a prime mover in building Fort Brainerd.

Darwin was one of five volunteers who helped put together Lake Ellen's first camp week, before buildings or ball fields had appeared in the mid-60s. Mike Rucinski will join me in telling that story and more in a sequel to this book, THE LEVITES, *Lake Ellen Camp Volunteers*. Mike was my friend when he was a teenager and I was his pastor. He left an engineering career to become Lake Ellen's first director and a pastor.

Fort Brainerd opened the way to an expanded vision for ministering to kids at Lake Ellen. Today, junior campers enjoy two rustic sites on Loon Lake. Fort Brainerd became North Point, and across the lake stand the teepees of Ojibwa Village. Volunteers built both centers.

Some sober saint will scan this book and ask, What's the point? Tall tales are an ancient campfire tradition, but the people in these stories are very real: Klaus Zeilke, Charles, Dick and Mark Murphy, Darwin Wilson, Jim and Shirley Carpenedo, Tim Green. They are friends who enriched my life. Their labor and gifts built a rustic campsite in the forest cathedral that has given good memories to hundreds of kids. That's point enough.

Lloyd Mattson
The Wordshed

Darwin Wilson and Lloyd Mattson
"Life is the sum of its friends and memories."

Trolls at Lake Ellen — 2004

Wordshed Mission Books and Audio Books:

Telling the stories of quiet heroes of the faith.

ALASKA: NEW LIFE FOR AN ANCIENT PEOPLE
Lloyd Mattson

ALASKA: A MAN FROM KANATAK
Paul Boskoffsky with Lloyd Mattson
Book and Audio with Music
Lloyd and Kevin Mattson

WALKING TO THE LIGHT, NOT AN EASY ROAD
G. Robert Nordling

BIGFOOT AND THE MICHIGAMME TROLLS
Book and Audio Book
Lloyd and Kevin Mattson

THE LEVITES, LAKE ELLEN VOLUNTEERS (2006)
Mike Rucinski and Lloyd Mattson

Available from the publisher:

The Wordshed
5118 Glendale Street ♦ Duluth, MN 55804
218/525-3266 ♦ wordshed@charter.net